MOUSE
WAS
MAD

Linda Urban

Illustrated by Henry Cole

sandpiper   Houghton Mifflin Harcourt   Boston • New York

Text copyright © 2009 by Linda Urban
Illustrations copyright © 2009 by Henry Cole

www.hmhco.com

The illustrations in this book were done in
watercolor, colored pencil, and ink on Arches hot press
watercolor paper.
The display type was set in Typography of Coop Black.
The text type was set in Billy.

The Library of Congress has cataloged the hardcover edition as follows:
Mouse was mad / Linda Urban; [illustrator] Henry Cole.
p. cm.
Summary: Mouse struggles to find the right way to express
his anger, modeling the behavior of Hare, Bear, Hedgehog,
and Bobcat, only to discover that his own way may be the
best way of all.
[1. Anger—Fiction. 2. Individuality—Fiction. 3. Mice—Fiction.
4. Animals—Fiction.] I. Cole, Henry, 1955—ill. II. Title.
PZ7.U637Mo 2009
[E]—dc22 2007045081

ISBN: 978-0-15-205337-6 hardcover
ISBN: 978-0-547-72750-9 paperback

Manufactured in China
SCP 17 16 15 14 13 12 11

4500693028

For Claire and Jack—L. U.

For my pals Anita and Debbie,
with affection—H. C.

Mouse was mad. **Hopping mad.**

"You look ridiculous," said Hare.
Mouse stopped hopping.

"Let me show you how to hop properly," said Hare,
who truly was a hopping whiz.

Mouse tried to hop like Hare.
Nothing doing.

Mouse

hop-hop-flopped—

SPLISH!—

into a mucky mud puddle.

Now Mouse was really mad.
Stomping mad.

"You call that stomping?" said Bear.

Mouse stopped stomping.

"Stomping, done right, should result in the shaking of trees and the rumbling of earth," said Bear. Bear stomped.

The trees shook, the earth rumbled.

Mouse tried to stomp like Bear.

The trees did not shake.

The earth did not rumble.

Mouse

stomp-stomp-flomped—

SPLUSH!—

into another mucky mud puddle.

Now Mouse was really, really mad.
Screaming mad.

"That's hardly a scream at all," said Bobcat.
Mouse stopped screaming.

"When I scream, you can hear it echo through the woods."
Bobcat screamed to prove his point. It echoed and echoed.

Mouse opened his mouth wide and let out
the loudest scream he could manage.
No echo.

He tried arching his back like Bobcat

but lost his balance and fell—

SPLOSH!—

into yet another mucky mud puddle.

Now Mouse was really, really, really mad.

Rolling-around-on-the-ground mad.

"Pull your feet in," said Hedgehog.

Mouse stopped rolling.

"The best rolling is achieved when the body is a perfect sphere." Hedgehog tucked in his nose and his feet and his hands. He was a perfect sphere.

Mouse tucked in his nose and his feet and his hands.

He was not a perfect sphere, but he was close.

He pulled in his tail

and rolled around and around—

SPLOOSH!—

into the muckiest mud puddle of all.

Now Mouse was really, really, really, really mad.
Standing-still mad.

Mouse did not hop. He did not stomp.

He did not scream or roll on the ground.

He stood very, very still.

"Impressive," said Hare.
"What control," said Bear.
"Are you breathing?"
asked Hedgehog.

Mouse took a deep breath.

He let his breath out.

Bobcat heard air whistle through Mouse's nose,

but he did not see Mouse move.

"Inspiring," said Bobcat.

Bobcat stood very still. He breathed deep and tried not to move.

"Your ears twitched," said Hare.
"Let me try." But he could not keep
his tail from wiggling.

Bear tried, but when he breathed deep, trees moved and the ground shook a little. Hedgehog came closest, but even he could not keep his bristles from bristling.

They stood together for a long time, breathing and trying to be still.

And then, Mouse realized he was no longer mad.

"I feel better now," said Mouse.

"You look better now," said Bear.

"But you need a bath," said Hedgehog.

"Good idea," said Mouse.

SPLASH!